WEiRDO5

TOTALLY WEIRD!

Scholastic Press
345 Pacific Highway Lindfield NSW 2070
An imprint of Scholastic Australia Pty Limited (ABN 11 000 614 577)
PO Box 579 Gosford NSW 2250
www.scholastic.com.au

Part of the Scholastic Group
Sydney • Auckland • New York • Toronto • London • Mexico City
• New Delhi • Hong Kong • Buenos Aires • Puerto Rico

First published by Scholastic Australia in 2015.
Text copyright © Anh Do, 2015.
Illustrations copyright © Jules Faber, 2015.

National Library of Australia Cataloguing-in-Publication entry
Creator: Do, Anh, author.
Title: Totally weird / Anh Do; illustrations by Jules Faber.
ISBN: 9781760155346 (paperback)
Series: Do, Anh. WeirDo; 5.
Target Audience: For primary school age.
Subjects: School camps—Juvenile fiction.
Friendship—Juvenile fiction. Talent shows—Juvenile fiction.
Other Creators/Contributors:
Faber, Jules, 1971- illustrator.
Dewey Number: A823.4

Typeset in Grenadine MVB, Push Ups and Lunch Box.

BLAH,
BLAH,
BLAH

Printed by RR Donnelley.
Scholastic Australia's policy, in association with
RR Donnelley, is to use papers that are renewable and
made efficiently from wood grown in responsibly managed
forests, so as to minimise its environmental footprint.

25 24 23 22 21   22 23 24 / 2

ANH DO

Illustrated by JULES FABER

WEiRDO5

TOTALLY WEIRD!

A SCHOLASTIC PRESS BOOK
FROM SCHOLASTIC AUSTRALIA

My best friend Henry **always** makes me 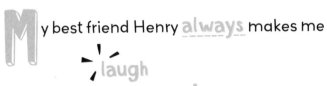 laugh out loud.

In fact, Henry makes everyone laugh out loud!

Henry was pecking at Bella's pencil case when the new kid arrived.

PECK!
PECK!

'Settle down, everyone,' said Miss Franklin.

WE HAVE A

NEW

STUDENT
JOINING
OUR CLASS . . .

'Come on in,' she said,
looking at the doorway.

Wow, I thought
to myself.

The new kid was

really,

REALLY . . .

HANS
SOME.

Hans Some?
That was his name?

WHAT'S
UP.

I couldn't believe this guy's actual name
was Hans Some!

'Hans, why don't you take a seat next to Weir Do?' said Miss Franklin.

Hans Some sat down beside me.

'So you're a weirdo?' he asked.

'That's me,' I said. 'It's my name. Weir, Do.'

'WeirDo,' Hans repeated. 'Lol.'

'Lol?' I asked.

'Yeah, lol,' he said.

'You want a lolly?'

'No, LOL. Don't you know?

  Like,

Laugh.

Out.

Loud,'

Hans explained s l o w l y.

'Oh, right. Lol,' I replied. 'Haha. I mean, *lol*.'

I wondered whether Bella knew what it meant.

I looked over at Bella and realised that

everyone

in my class was staring at Hans.

Even Henry!

Hans was

just

so . . .

handsome.

And what a cool name! It was so much better than Weir Do! If only I was Hans Some!

This new guy is totally perfect.

His teeth are so white and sparkly and straight.

They could use him in an ad for toothpaste.

USE OUR TOOTHPASTE AND HAVE PERFECT TEETH, JUST LIKE HANS SOME!

perfect!

While my teeth are ...

well ...

not so white

or sparkly

or straight.

NOT perfect!

Cornflake!

His hair is so shiny and smooth.

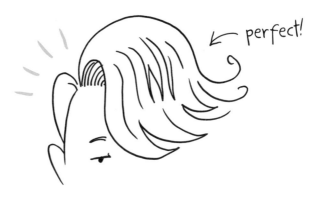
perfect!

While mine almost always looks like
I just crawled out of bed.

bird →
Cornflake
NOT
perfect!

15

His shoes look really cool and new.

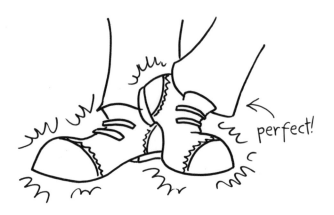

perfect!

While mine used to belong to my big sister, Sally.

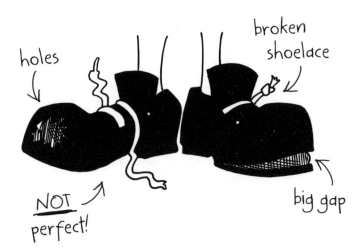

holes

broken shoelace

NOT perfect!

big gap

And even his handwriting is _super neat_!

It's like a computer did it!

perfect! →

My name is Hans Some.

Yes. Hans Some.

Hi! I'm weir.
Weir Do!

NOT perfect!

← Cornflake!

While mine looks like my little brother Roger did it!

Oh man, this guy has everything! Including the best name around!

I wouldn't be surprised if his nickname was Awe, as in AWE-SOME!

When the recess bell rang, Henry waddled over to us. He was still in pigeon-mode.

It made me laugh!

I looked at Hans. He didn't even lol!

COO! COO!

But Henry was hilarious!

'Is this guy your B.F.F.?' Hans asked me.

'Oh no, he's my best friend,' I said.

BFF *MEANS* BEST FRIENDS FOREVER. GOT IT?

Oh man, I don't get this new guy at all!

MAKE-
OVER!

CHAPTER 2

Hans Some is <u>so</u> cool.
I thought maybe I could be cool, too.

I found my sister Sally in her room, playing with Blockhead and FiDo.

WHAT'S UP?

WHAT'S UP?

HMM . . .

THE SKY.

Lol!

'Lol?' Sally repeated.

'It means Laugh Out Loud,' I said. 'Don't you know?'

'I know what LOL means,' said Sally. 'I've just never heard it said out loud before.'

OH . . .

Was I the last person on earth to find out what lol meant?

I bet there were cavemen who knew what it meant.

'Do you know what BFF means?' I asked Sally.

'Of course. **B**est **F**riends **F**orever,' she replied.
'Like these two!'

Even Blockhead knew what it meant!
And now he was laughing at me!

Something needed
to be done . . .

Before dinner, I decided to go through my clothes to try and find myself a new look.

Maybe a makeover was what I needed.

New Look #1

Hmm,
I don't think so...

New Look #2 →

Umm, not sure.

New Look #3

No way!

I decided to try out New Look #2 with my family.

My pants were so tight I couldn't even bend my knees. Sitting down wasn't easy!

'Hi Weir,' said Mum. 'You look different.'

'I thought it was about time I ... um ... changed my look a bit,' I explained.

'I can help you with that!' said Dad.

I WAS QUITE A FASHIONABLE GUY IN MY DAY. PEOPLE COULDN'T STOP STARING AT ME WHEN I WALKED DOWN THE STREET.

'That's true,' Mum agreed.

'People ALWAYS stared!'

YO.

WHAT IS
THAT GUY
WEARING!?

'*Okaaaaay,*' I said. I'd seen photos of Dad when he was younger.

This could get really bad! But I figured it was

worth a shot.

After we'd eaten, Dad went

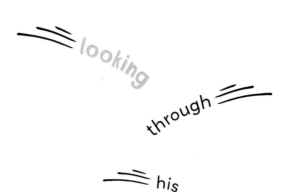

looking through his drawers.

He picked out a <u>brand new</u> outfit for me.

When I was ready, I strutted out . . .

But no-one liked my outfit!
Not even Blockhead or Fido!

I guess I did look pretty silly!

Everyone started laughing . . . except me.
I said something else.

'Lol?' asked Mum.

'Lol?' asked Dad.

'Lol?' asked Granddad.

'Yep, LOL,' I said. 'The first letters of "Laugh out loud." It's the way all the cool kids talk.'

'Is that so?' said Dad.

THEN I THINK
I MIGHT GO
OUTSIDE TO SMB!

I realised then that it was much more fun to just laugh than to say 'lol'.

CHAPTER 3

Everyone in class liked Hans Some. They liked him a lot.

Especially the girls ...

We were all really excited about class CAMP, which was coming up in just a few days.

Hans was telling everyone about the camp
he went on with his old school, and how he
rescued five kids from the river after their
canoe turned over.

THANK YOU, HANS SOME!

Our whole class thought it was awesome.

He also told us how he rescued a whole family of possums from a falling tree after a lightning strike.

SQUEEEEAK, SQUEAK!

And then he told us about how he stopped
an angry big brown bear ...
by singing him a lullaby.

Miss Franklin asked the class for volunteer team leaders. 'We'll need four people

who know a lot

about camping,' she said.

'They'll lead the two teams in the

CAMP KANGAROO
CHALLENGE!'

 Hans put his hand straight up,

as well as Bella .

I'd **never** been camping before ...
but I didn't want to miss out.

Especially if Bella was going to be a leader!

MISS!
MISS!

Miss Franklin made Bella and Hans the leaders of one group...

and me and Wendy the leaders of the other group.

Oh, man! What had I got myself into? I knew nothing about camping! I hoped Wendy knew more than I did!

ON YOUR
MARKS...

CHAPTER 4

We were all pretty excited when we pulled up at

CAMP KANGAROO!

After we met Ranger Jack, our CAMP CAPTAIN, we split up into our teams and prepared for the challenges!

Bella and Hans were the leaders of

\ | | | / ,
the blue team.
/ | | | \ \

Wendy and I were the leaders of

\ | | | / ,
the red team.
/ | | | \ \

Everyone wore coloured bandanas
to show which team they belonged to.

Team Red—
← red
bandana

When Hans tied his bandana **around his neck** ...

Team Blue—
blue bandana

everyone copied him ...

Toby

Bella

Jenny

There were going to be

five challenges

over two days.

CAMP KANGAROO	WINNER
1. Tent building: 5 points	
2. Hole digging: 5 points	
3. Obstacle course: 5 points	
4. Canoe race: 5 points	
5. FINALE Song Contest: 5 points	

The first challenge was tent building!

I'd never put up a tent before ... but I told my team to trust me.

ON YOUR MARKS, GET SET. GO!

But that wasn't true. In fact, I got myself **completely tangled** up...

OOPS!

I have **no idea** what went wrong!

Luckily, Wendy and Henry were able to free me ...

And with me out of the way, they were able to get the tent up **properly** ...

...a second **after** Hans and Bella's team.

'We have our first challenge winner,' announced Ranger Jack. **'Team Blue!'**

Bella and Hans turned to each other and high-fived.

CAMP KANGAROO	WINNER
1. Tent building: 5 points	BLUE
2. Hole digging: 5 points	
3. Obstacle course: 5 points	
4. Canoe race: 5 points	
5. FINALE Song Contest: 5 points	

The second challenge was hole digging.

Two against two—it was

ME + WENDY

VS.

BELLA + HANS.

I'd only ever dug a hole at the beach with a plastic spade, and I never even finished it because a crab

chased

me

away.

Did you know that crabs are fast?

 REALLLLY FAST!

B Fold line B over
to meet line A

But I told Wendy and my team to trust me.

DON'T WORRY, I'VE GOT THIS!

ON YOUR MARKS, GET SET, GO!

I grabbed one of the shovels
and started digging madly.

WHEEE

DIG
DIG   DIG

Thing is, Wendy and I were both

digging so madly,

we weren't watching where the dirt was going!

All the dirt I was digging was flying over my head and into the hole Wendy was digging ...

and all the dirt she was digging was going over her head and landing back in my hole ...

I think I heard a couple of wombats laughing at how badly I was digging.

It wasn't until I heard Bella call out 'Done!'
that I stopped what I was doing and looked up.

HUH?

'Winner!' called Ranger Jack. He held
up Bella's hand and Team Blue cheered.

Oops.

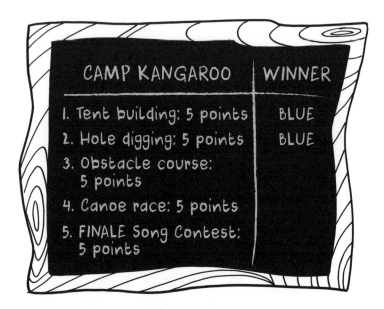

CAMP KANGAROO	WINNER
1. Tent building: 5 points	BLUE
2. Hole digging: 5 points	BLUE
3. Obstacle course: 5 points	
4. Canoe race: 5 points	
5. FINALE Song Contest: 5 points	

GO BLUE! TOTALLY COOL!

Bella and Hans were making a
really good team...

And I'd done nothing but let my team down.

'Sorry, guys,' I told them. 'I guess I don't know as much about camping as I thought I did. In fact, I don't really know anything at all...'

'That's okay, Weir,' said Wendy.

'Let's all work really hard together and try
to win the next challenge,' added Henry.

'Deal,' I said.

GOO

OOOOOOOO
RED!

There were three parts to the obstacle course—the tyres, the balance beam and the mud pit.

A *whole* team had to make it over the finish line to win the race.

CAMP KANGAROO

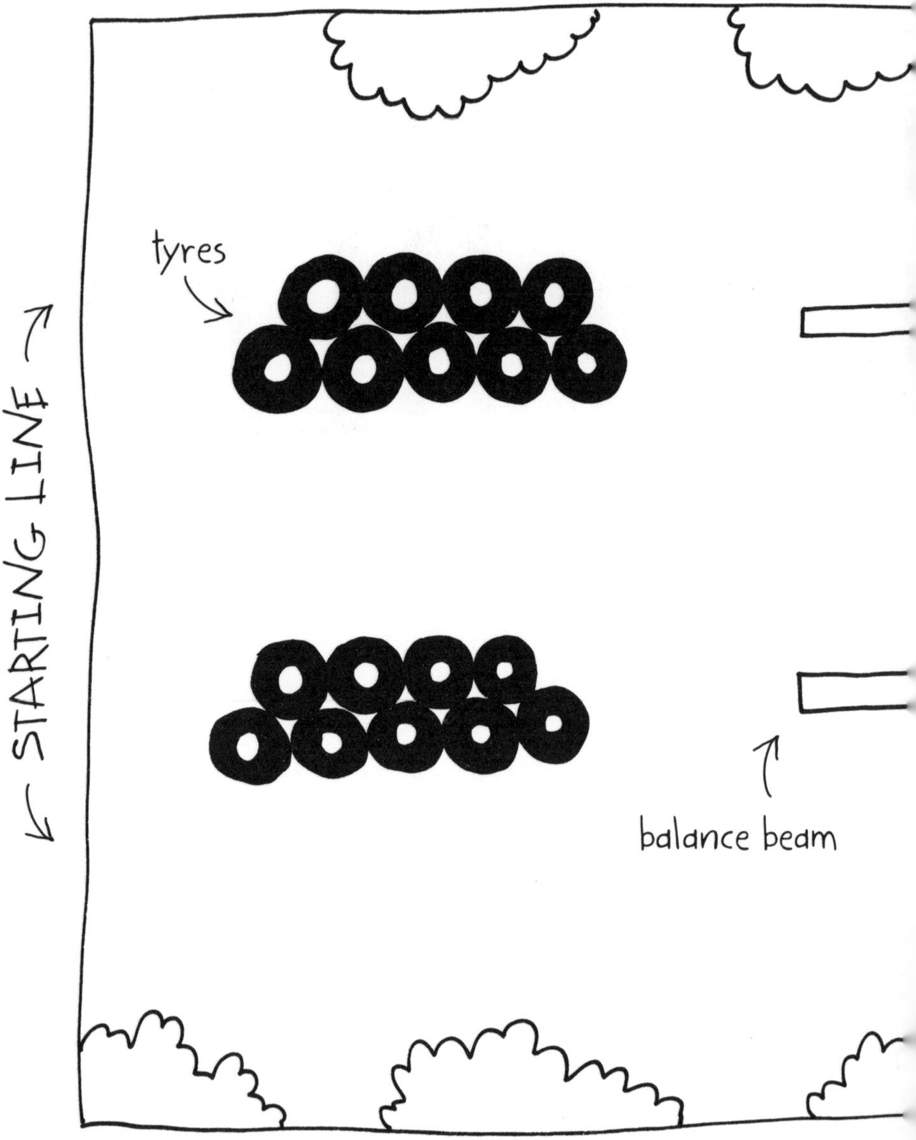

tyres

← STARTING LINE →

balance beam

OBSTACLE COURSE MAP

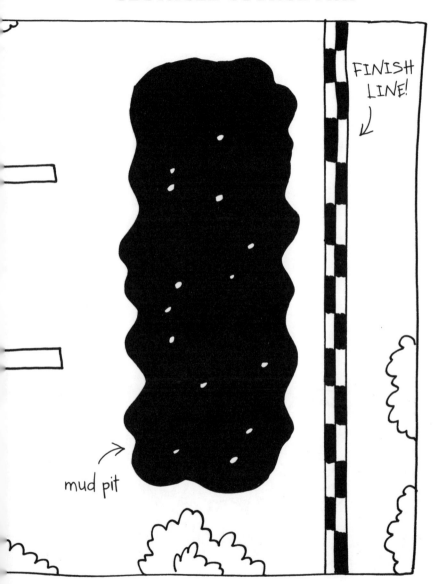

FINISH LINE!

mud pit

'We can do this,' Henry urged Team Red.

'We sure can,' agreed Wendy. 'We can make a comeback. We just need to work together.'

TEAM RED V

Team Red and Team Blue gathered at the starting line. You could tell we both really wanted to win this one.

S. TEAM BLUE

ON YOUR MARKS, GET SET, GO!

Wendy is the class hopscotch champ. So to get over the tyres, all we had to do was follow her moves.

HOP   HOP   HOP

She was amazing! The rest of us followed fast behind her.

I spotted Hans darting out as well. In fact, he was SO fast that he overtook Wendy and was already starting to make his way over the balance beam!

SWOOSH

Man, this guy had THE COOLEST name, plus he was so good-looking, plus he was REALLY, REALLY FAST!

And it looked like Bella *really* liked him . . .

Team Red was over the tyres and we were all slowly making our way over the balance beam . . .

...when I noticed that Hans was *SO* far ahead, he was almost through the mud pit!

Really?

He was **superfast!**

And he even looked cool covered in mud!

Hans was already over the finish line ...

but his teammates were all the way back at the tyres!

FIRST TEAM OVER THE FINISH LINE WINS! YOU ALL HAVE TO MAKE IT OVER.

Bella, who'd almost caught up to Hans, ran back to help Toby Hogan. Toby had

and fallen face-first

into the middle of a tyre.

OOOOOF!

Even though Toby was on Team Blue, I just couldn't leave Bella to pull him out of the tyre by herself.

So I ran back to help her.

ONE . . .
TWO . . .
THREE . . .
PULL!

WHOOSH!

Once Toby, Jenny and Mary were okay and back on the balance beam, I rejoined the race and

dived into the mud pit.

SPLOSH!

Wriggling through mud is

SO MUCH FUN!

TOLD YOU SO.

We all swam through and came out looking like swamp monsters!

Before we knew it, Ranger Jack had blown his whistle.

'And the first team over the finish line is ...'

We'd done it!

We'd worked as a team and **won** the race!

WOOOHOOOOOO!

GO TEAM!

WE DID IT!

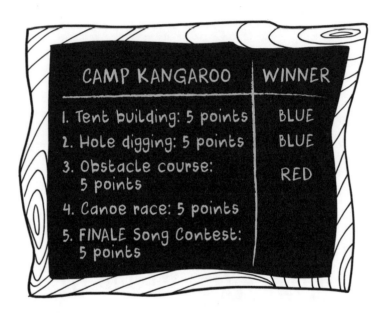

CAMP KANGAROO	WINNER
1. Tent building: 5 points	BLUE
2. Hole digging: 5 points	BLUE
3. Obstacle course: 5 points	RED
4. Canoe race: 5 points	
5. FINALE Song Contest: 5 points	

Bella jogged over the line with Toby
and the rest of Team Blue.

Toby was so happy, he ran over and did a
massive belly flop in the mud pit.

He made such a big splash that mud flew out of the mud pit ...

all over Bella ...

all over Henry...

all over me ...

and hit Ranger Jack right in the face!

SPLASH!

It was so funny!

'Lol!' I said. 'I mean, HAHAHAHAHAHAA!' And
my whole team cracked up laughing with me!

CHAPTER 5

Our first night at camp was **heaps of fun.**

We **toasted marshmallows** by the camp fire and made each other **laugh**.

Henry told some **jokes** ...

WHAT'S A GHOSTS FAVOURITE DESSERT?

I-SCREEEEEEEEEEEEEAM!

AAARGHH!!!

Then **Clare** got up and wobbled her head, which made her **pigtails spin** in different directions.

Joey Keenan made his legs **wobble** really fast.

Everyone in Team Red is really good at something!

WOBBLE

WOBBLE

Mullet can make his face look like just about any animal.

goldfish

pug

frog

horse

Even **Blake Green** has a **thumb trick** that no-one else can do.

As I watched my team, I realised I had been trying to do everything myself when I had a **whole TEAM** who could have helped me.

106

After dinner, we worked on our team song for our final challenge at

THE CAMP KANGAROO Song Contest.

The show was on the next afternoon, so we needed all the practise we could get!

LET'S DO THIS
TOGETHER!

Everyone helped come up with a song that we all really liked!

TEAM RED, YOU SOUND GREAT. WENDY AND WEIR, YOU MAKE TERRIFIC TEAM LEADERS.

THANKS, MISS.

I was pretty sure Team Blue was having heaps of fun, too. Not that I could see them. They were camped with Ranger Jack on the other side of the river.

Hans Some was probably in the middle of telling everyone really cool ghost stories.

WOW, HANS.
THAT WAS THE COOLEST
GHOST STORY EVER!

I wondered what song they'd come up with for the final challenge.

Hans Some had already told us that he was an amazing singer. His voice would probably lead his team to victory.

TO YOOUUUUUUU

Maybe Hans and Bella would do a duet ...

We had another big day ahead. There was the canoe race, then the final challenge ...

Beating Team Blue was going to be tough!

CHAPTER 6

Team Red was READY for the canoe race.

GO TEAM RED!

There were five of us in each canoe. Bella was at the back of Team Blue's canoe and Hans was up front, like me.

Hans and I looked over at each other.

HI, HANS!

I waved a little too hard and **lost** my balance!

WHOA!

Luckily, Henry stopped me from
falling in the **river**!

We had to row **all the way** up to the other end of Camp Kangaroo, where Ranger Jack would be waiting for the <u>winner</u>!

Miss Franklin stood by the side of the river, about to **start** the race.

READY, SET, GO!

Team Blue was off to a flying start.
They **whizzed** ahead like a speedboat!

'Come on, Red!' I called.

'Row, row, row,' Wendy and I chanted.

Team Red rowed together perfectly.

ROW,
ROW,
ROW!

We darted through the water and started catching up to Team Blue!

'Row, row, row!' we chanted. And, in moments, we'd caught up!

Hans looked worried. He was **shouting** out **lots of orders** to his team, but it wasn't really helping them.

COME ON, **ROW HARDER!**

'Row, row, row!' we chanted.

I couldn't believe it—we were out in front and getting a pretty good lead!

ROW, ROW, ROW.

Meanwhile, Hans was rowing like **crazy**. He was paddling like an **angry duck**!

← very angry duck

He was rowing **SO** hard ... and **SO** much harder than everyone else in his team ...

that Team Blue's canoe started going in *circles*!

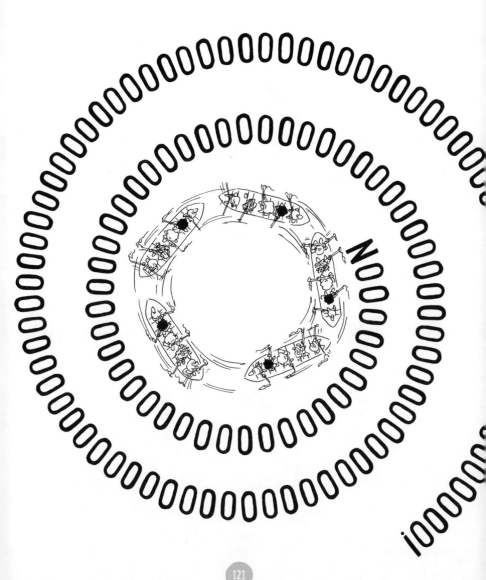

Team Red could see the finish line! There was
Ranger Jack!

BRRRRRRRRRRRRRRRR!

We'd won! Team Red had won!

YEAH!

CHAPTER 7

The scores were __even__!

CAMP KANGAROO	WINNER
1. Tent building: 5 points	BLUE
2. Hole digging: 5 points	BLUE
3. Obstacle course: 5 points	RED
4. Canoe race: 5 points	RED
5. FINALE Song Contest: 5 points	

BLUE	RED
⬇	⬇
10 points	10 points

It was all going to come down to the final show!

Our families had come to CAMP KANGAROO to watch our performances.

Mum, Dad, Granddad, Sally and Roger waved to me from the audience. Even Fido and Blockhead were there!

Team Red was up first.

We ran onto the stage and I stood in front of the mic with Wendy. I smiled back at my team.

I looked down at the mic and realised there was something I needed to do.

I untied my bandana from around my neck ... and wrapped it around my forehead. It was time to be myself again.

Everyone else in Team Red moved their bandanas, too.

We were ready!

'Okay, team, let's do it!' I called.

'Three,
two,
one . . .'

'GO RED,
GO BLUE!

STAY TRUE,
BE YOU!

Miss Franklin helped us on the guitar
and Henry played the bongo drum.

upside-down
ice-cream tub

AND NO-ONE ELSE!

Team Red sounded awesome! We were having

SO MUCH FUN TOGETHER!

The crowd was cheering and they even started joining in!

BE YOURSELF AND NO-ONE ELSE!

It was time for each of us to do our own crazy dance move...

which really got the crowd going.

Everyone knows how great my dad is at dancing!

washing machine move

And everyone knows Roger loves to dance!

break-dancing Roger

And then it was time for the big finish— we all made funny faces.

The crowd loved it!

THANK YOU!

THANKS, TEAM RED!
AND NOW, COULD YOU PLEASE
GIVE A **HUGE** CHEER
FOR TEAM BLUE!
HERE THEY ARE WITH
THEIR SONG . . .
TOTALLY COOL!

Team Blue ran onto the stage. Hans had the microphone. I prepared myself for his amazing voice...

But guess what?

SO GOOO

YIKES!

He was
TERRIBLE!

It was worse than the noise Roger makes when
he slams the toilet seat on his thing!

OOOOWWWW!

OOOL!

In fact, the whole team seemed to be **covering their ears!**

And Hans just kept on ~~singing~~!

screeching!

COOOL

141

The audience didn't know what to do.
It was a disaster!

Bella tried to
share the mic
with Hans,
but he was
too busy
screeching
to notice her!

With his voice, he should have been singing
So Cruel, not So Cool!

I looked at Henry. We wanted
to help Team Blue!

We crawled across the stage
with Team Red's mic.

We jumped up when we reached Bella.

Soon we had the rest of Team Blue at the mic,
singing Totally Cool. All of Team Red joined in.
Hans was still screeching his lungs out, but now
the rest of his team had a chance to be heard!

144

anger Jack announced that Team Red were the winners of the Song Contest, which meant we'd won the CAMP KANGAROO CHALLENGE!

YEAH!

GO CAMP KANGAROO!

We all had <u>such a great time</u> at camp, it was sad to say goodbye.

SWAMP MONSTER SAD

Just as I was climbing into the car, I heard someone calling my name.

WEIR!
WEIR!

It was Bella.

WEIR!

'Thanks SO much for helping
our team earlier,' she said.
'We really needed it.'

'I just wanted to save everyone's eardrums!'
I said, and Bella laughed.

I had something I wanted to ask her ...

SO, UM, BELLA,
IS HANS SOME
YOUR ...
BFF?

'No,' Bella said with a giggle. 'He's not my BFF. He's far too bossy.'

Phew.

For my **mum** and **dad**, who encouraged me to be myself, even though I was a bit **weird**

FROM ANH

ACKNOWLEDGEMENTS

FROM JULES

For all my **fabulous** friends
at Casuarina Steiner School
in Coffs Harbour.
What a community!

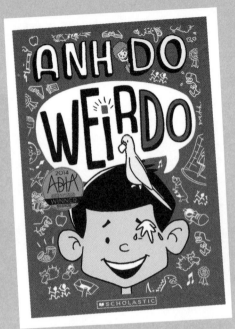

AUSTRALIAN BOOK INDUSTRY AWARDS WINNER!

Book 1

GOT IT!

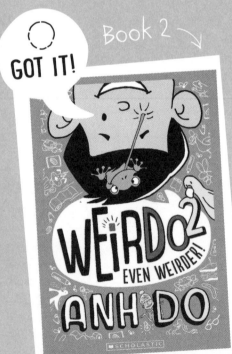

Book 2

GOT IT!

Book 3

GOT IT!

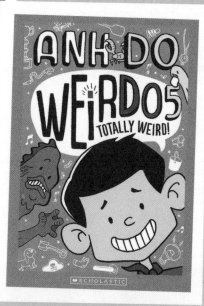

STAY
TUNED!